# AFLOAT

Levine Querido acknowledges the Native peoples, tribes, and nations of what is now known as the United States, and the First Nations, Métis, and Inuit of the lands now known as Canada. We extend our respect to the First Nations Peoples around the world and recognize their continued connection to the land, waters, sky, and culture.

This is an Arthur A. Levine book
Published by Levine Querido
www.levinequerido.com · info@levinequerido.com

LQ
LEVINE QUERIDO

Levine Querido is distributed by Chronicle Books, LLC

Originally published in Australia in 2024 by Hardie Grant Children's Publishing
Text copyright © 2024 by Kirli Saunders
Illustrations copyright © 2024 by Freya Blackwood

All rights reserved

Library of Congress Control Number: 2024942333
ISBN 9781646145072

Printed and bound in China

Published in March 2025
First Printing

＝

Roam the water with me.
We are here to learn.

Here to spin wisdom, to grow.

Walk a little further with me.
We are here to collect the vines.

Here to find the rushes,
to fuse the fibers.

To roll between finger and thumb.
To yarn.

Take the string with me.
We are here to knot and loop.

Here to form bonds,
to make ties.

Pull them close with me.
We are here to meld and fold.

To weld oneness.
To unite.

Push out next to me.
We are here to brave the storm.

Stand up next to me.

We are here to fly,
here to shape this world together.

To thrive.

*Afloat* was written for Indigenous, Native, and First Nations Peoples across the globe—it's for my community, it's for the weavers of the world, and for everyone who is with us on our journey. The text pays homage to cultural and plant knowledge handed down to us, by our Elders. It honors our women especially.

The story follows an Elder, teaching gathering and weaving practices to a child. As they continue, more people join them, until all are united in their efforts to move towards a promising future where this knowledge is deeply known and valued. At the heart of *Afloat* is a metaphor of weaving together, to form a raft, to brave a storm as one.

*Afloat* sits in the broader global political context of the climate crisis. It is written for this time of rising seas, where First Nations, Native, and Indigenous peoples particularly are dispossessed of their homelands and displaced.

*Afloat* is written with the knowledge that connection to our homelands, our Country, is paramount to our identity. It is written with love, and the intention to unify, and to make change, so our knowledge can continue to be connected to Land, Sky and Sea, and we can continue to practice our Culture, and share it with our children, keeping it alive for all times.

I am deeply grateful to Freya, for her illustrations which capture these big ideas so heartily. And for the time we've spent slowly, yarning and weaving, shaping this story.

And to my weaving teachers, my Elders, my sissys, Mum, and Kylie Caldwell, always, always, thank you.

– Kirli